The Best Thanksgiving ~Ever!~

The Best Thanksgiving Ever!

by **Teddy Slater**

Illustrated by **Ethan Long**

Cartwheel
·B·O·O·K·S·®

Scholastic Inc.

New York Toronto London Auckland Sydney

Mexico City New Delhi Hong Kong Buenos Aires

ISBN-13: 978-0-439-87390-1
ISBN-10: 0-439-87390-8

Text copyright © 2005 by Teddy Slater.
Illustrations copyright © 2005 by Ethan Long.

All rights reserved. Published by Scholastic Inc.
SCHOLASTIC, CARTWHEEL BOOKS, and associated logos
are trademarks and/or registered trademarks of Scholastic Inc.

10 9 8 7 6 5 4 3 2 1   7 8 9 10 11/0
BOOK DESIGN BY JENNIFER RINALDI WINDAU
Printed in the U.S.A.
This edition first printing, October 2007

For Judy Bernstein and Ken Goldman
—T.S.

To my big, crazy, loving family
—E.L.

It's late in November,
the blue sky is clear,
and Thanksgiving Day
is finally here.

This year, the Turkeys are hosting the feast.

The whole family's coming—a dozen, at least.

Aunt Biddy from Denver
arrived late last night,

with Grandma and Grandpa,
and Great-uncle Dwight.

Tom gets out the dust mop,
Tess gets out the broom.

All in a flurry, they fly
through the room.

The kinfolk pitch in to prepare the huge meal.
With so many helpers, it's not a big deal.

The pie's in the oven.
The table is set.
This looks like the very best
Thanksgiving yet.

Riiiinnnng! goes the doorbell.
It's Granddaddy Beau,
Grandmother Tillie,
and sweet baby Mo.

Right behind them
comes Mo's mama, Lee,
with Uncle Pierre
and Cousin Marie.

So many hugs and
so many kisses.

So many
"Happy Thanksgiving"
wishes.

The Turkeys are thankful
for all that they've got.

For some it's a little.
For some it's a lot.

Tillie gives thanks
for the blue sky above.
Grandpa is thankful
for Grandmother's love.

Dwight's full of thanks
for the cool autumn weather.
Aunt Biddy gives thanks that
the whole clan's together.

They all gather 'round
for a Thanksgiving song.

Come giggle. Come gobble.
Come sing along.

Tom strums his banjo.
Lee toots her horn.

Everyone's thankful . . .

. . . for Thanksgiving corn!